MONSTER,
BE GOOD!

pictures by
Natalie Marshall

BLUE APPLE

DON'T BE SCARED!

You are in charge of the monsters.

If you tell them how to behave, they will listen.

If a monster is noisy,
whisper in its ear,

"BE QUIET!"

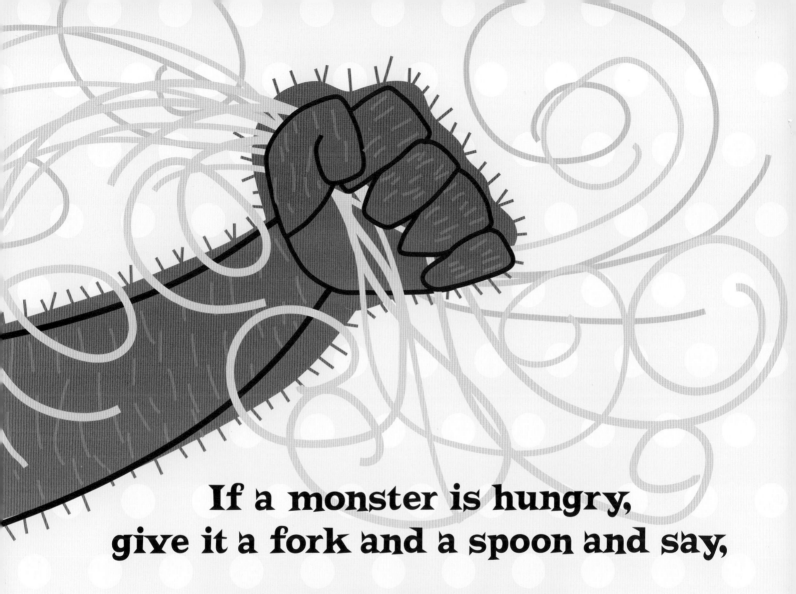

If a monster is hungry,
give it a fork and a spoon and say,

"CHEW YOUR FOOD!"

If a monster
is selfish,
say,

"TAKE TURNS!"

If a monster is mean,
walk away and say,

"GOOD-BYE!"

If a monster scares you,
scare it back and say,

"**BOO!**"

If a monster makes a mess,
say,

"CLEAN UP!"

If a monster is wild, give it a time-out and say,

"SIT STILL!"

If a monster is tired
and grumpy,
send it to bed and say,

"GO TO SLEEP!"

And if the monster
asks nicely,
kiss it and say …